Usborne English

Level 2

Theseus
and the
Minotaur

Retold by Anthony Marks

Illustrated by Matteo Pincelli

English language consultant: Peter Viney

Contents

You can listen to the story online here:
usborne.com/theseusaudio

Theseus was the prince of Athens, a great city in Greece, long ago. Theseus's father was King Aegeus, and the people of Athens loved their wise king and his brave and handsome son.

Athens was near the sea, and ships sailed there from many other cities, near and far. But there was one ship that nobody in the city ever wanted to see.

Every year, a big ship with a black sail arrived from the island of Crete. King Minos of Crete was a powerful, angry man. Everyone knew that below his palace, he kept a monster. Its name was the Minotaur.

It was like a giant, with the head of an enormous black bull and long horns – but that wasn't the worst thing about it. The monster killed and ate people, and it was always hungry.

King Minos's ships and his soldiers were far more powerful than the Athenians. They defeated the Athenians in a war, and then Minos began to make his terrible demands. Every year, the Athenians had to send seven young men and seven young women to Crete. They never came back, and everyone knew why.

Each time the ship appeared with its black sail, the streets of Athens filled with the sound of crying.

Everyone had to go to the open square in the middle of the city. The king's soldiers took fourteen names from two enormous pots, and read them in a loud voice. One by one, fourteen young people stepped forward. Sometimes their parents shouted, "No! Not my son!" or "Please, not my daughter!" but they knew that they had no choice. The fourteen young people had to leave the city and go to the ship.

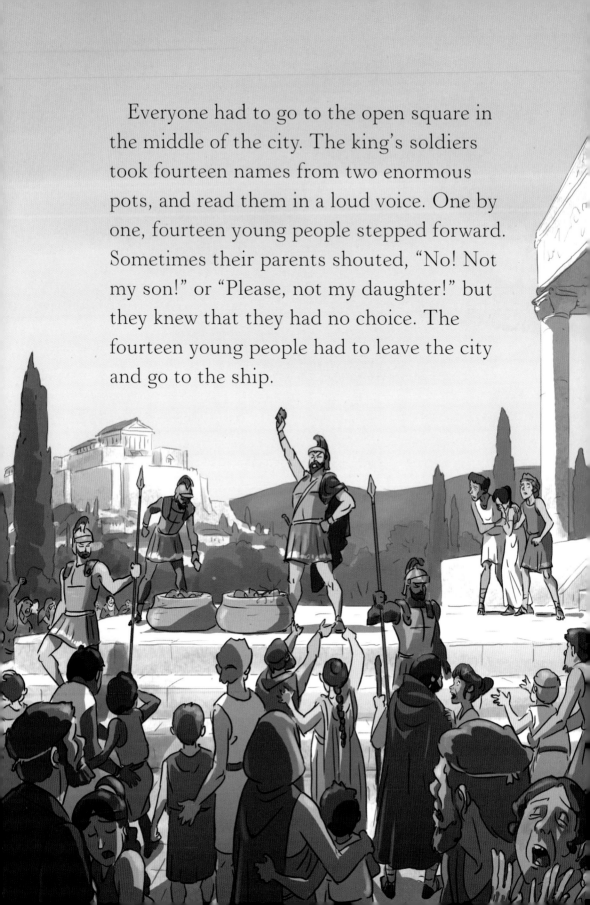

For two years, Theseus watched unhappily each time the young people left for Crete. Then, during the third year, he went to his father Aegeus.

"Why do you always agree to Minos's demands?" he said. "You are sending our young people to Crete where they will die. You know that."

"What can I do?" asked Aegeus. "If I refuse, Minos will attack us again and we will *all* die."

"Father, does my name ever go into the pots?" asked Theseus. "Tell me the truth."

Aegeus looked at the ground. "It does not. You are a prince, and you are my only son. I need you here with me."

"That's not fair," said Theseus. "It's not right. You must let me go to Crete this year. I will defeat the Minotaur and bring our people home safely."

Aegeus looked at him. "How will you do that? Do you think Minos hasn't tried? He is afraid of his bull-monster. His soldiers couldn't kill it. Instead, it killed them."

Now he has built an enormous maze under the palace. It's called the Labyrinth. When you go into the maze, it's almost dark except for a few torches on the walls. You see paths to the left and paths to the right. You turn this way and then that way, and soon you are lost. You can't escape. Then, from the middle of the maze, you hear the roars of the Minotaur... and that is the last thing you will ever hear."

It was a warm day, but Theseus suddenly felt cold. "That's horrible," he said. "But Father, I have to go. Someone has to stop the killing."

Aegeus looked at him sadly. "You are brave, I know that – but you are all I have."

"And the others?" asked Theseus. "Some of them are the only sons or daughters that their parents have, too. I promise you, Father, I will come back. We will *all* come back."

A few days later, the Cretan ship arrived. This year was different. Everyone in Athens knew about Theseus's promise.

When he saw the ship, Theseus pointed to its black sail. "Listen, here is another promise. If I kill the Minotaur, I will come home to Athens on that ship. If I am safe. I will put up a white sail instead of the black one. When you see the white sail, you will know the good news."

Then Theseus and the other young people stepped onto the ship. They sailed away, and Aegeus and the Athenians watched silently. "We have to do this," they said. "It's our only chance."

When the ship reached Crete, King Minos's soldiers immediately put Theseus and the other young Athenians in a prison in the palace.

That night, the Athenians had a surprise visitor. It was Minos's daughter, the princess Ariadne. Ariadne was unhappy on Crete. She was afraid of her cruel and angry father. She hated the sound of the Minotaur's roars at night. The young Athenians were the same age as her. She felt terrible because they were going to die.

She wanted to help them, and she wanted to escape from the island. She came back to speak to Theseus the next night, and the night after. Each time they spoke, she liked him more. Theseus liked her too, and he told her his plan.

"Please, promise to take me with you when you leave the island. If you do that, I will help you to defeat the Minotaur. Then we can rescue your friends," she told him.

"Is that safe for you?" asked Theseus. "What will happen if your father finds out?"

"He will punish me," said Ariadne. "He might even kill me. That is why you have to take me away with you."

The next day, Minos's soldiers told Theseus, "The King has decided. Tomorrow is the day when the first of you will go to meet the Minotaur."

"I will be the first," said Theseus. "I'm ready."

That evening, Ariadne came to the prison. "Come with me, quickly," she said. "My father's soldiers are sleeping and nobody will see us. I will take you to the Labyrinth."

When they reached the entrance, Ariadne showed him the enormous, heavy door. Theseus stepped forward and began to open it.

"Wait," Ariadne said. She gave him a sword. "You will need this to kill the Minotaur. Remember, the monster is very strong. You must wait until it is tired and confused before you try to kill it."

Next, she gave him a ball of thread. "Fix one end to the door when you go in. Keep the ball with you and unroll it when you go through the maze. Leave a line of thread all the way behind you. Go in as far as you can. You may be lucky. It's night time and the Minotaur may be asleep."

"I really hope so," said Theseus.

Ariadne added, "When you have killed the monster, turn around and follow the thread back to the entrance." They said goodbye. "I will wait for you here," said Ariadne. "I have spoken to the sailors. The ship will be ready for us. We will rescue your friends, and then we can leave. Good luck!"

"Thank you," said Theseus. "I will need it," he thought.

Quietly, he pushed the door further open and went inside. Then he closed the door and fixed one end of the ball of thread to it. It was almost dark in the Labyrinth, and almost silent. Sometimes, a burning torch on the wall gave a little light. The air was warm and there was a horrible smell, but he couldn't hear the Minotaur.

Further and further he went, as quietly as possible. He let the thread unroll behind him. In the middle of the maze, he found the monster. It was lying on its side, and it was asleep. In the torchlight, it looked powerful and dark and wicked. Its bull's head was enormous.

Theseus slowly moved closer. Then the Minotaur woke with a loud roar and jumped up to attack.

Theseus caught its long horns and
jumped right over its body. Again and again
the monster attacked, roaring and shaking
its cruel horns from side to side. It was very
strong, but Theseus was much lighter and
he could move faster. He waited for a chance
to use his sword. He was getting tired, but
the Minotaur was moving more slowly now.

Finally the Minotaur ran straight towards him, but at the last minute, Theseus jumped to one side. The Minotaur couldn't stop, and its head hit the hard stone wall. It fell to the floor and roared for the last time. Theseus took out his sword and killed the monster.

After the fight, Theseus was exhausted, but he knew he couldn't rest. He needed to get away from the Labyrinth before Minos's soldiers found him. He followed the thread back to the entrance. Finally he pulled open the doors, climbed out and fell onto his knees in the fresh night air. Ariadne was waiting for him.

"Theseus, you're alive! And the Minotaur..?"

It was hard for Theseus to speak. Then he said, "Yes. The Minotaur is dead."

"You're so brave!" she said. She put her arms around him.

As soon as Theseus could walk, he and
Ariadne rescued the young Athenians
from the prison, and they all hurried to the
ship. They brought Ariadne's young sister
Phaedra with them, too. "I can't leave her
in this horrible place," Ariadne said. "Who
knows what will happen to her?" The sailors
were waiting and the ship was ready. They
sailed away into the dark before Minos
could find out about the Minotaur.

The next day, the Athenians sailed as far from Crete as they could. The sun was hot and they were soon thirsty, but they had no fresh water on the ship.

"You know we left Crete in a hurry. We couldn't bring water. We didn't have time," said one of the sailors.

"We can sail to the next island and find some there," said Ariadne. "We must be safe from my father by now."

That evening, they stopped at the beautiful island of Naxos. They were all exhausted and they needed to rest. First they found water, then they made a fire and cooked some food. Then they slept under the trees.

Early the next morning, the sailors woke Theseus. "There's a storm coming," they said. "We must leave for Athens immediately!"

"Quickly! Go back to the ship!" Theseus shouted to his friends. They woke and hurried to the boat. Everyone was worried and confused.

"Is Ariadne here?" shouted Theseus. "The Cretan princess?"

"Yes," said one of the sailors. "I've seen her. She's on the ship already." The wind filled the sail and they started moving.

The wind grew stronger, and Theseus soon saw his mistake. The young woman on the ship was Phaedra, not Ariadne. Ariadne was still on Naxos.

"Turn around," demanded Theseus. "We must rescue her!"

"We can't," said the sailors. "It's too dangerous!"

Ariadne woke up on Naxos. Where was everybody? Then she saw the ship, far out on the sea. She was first frightened and then angry. How could Theseus leave her like this? How could he be so cruel?

She fell on her knees and reached up to the sky. "Punish them!" she shouted. "I saved them from the Minotaur! How could they forget me so soon?"

Hours later, the storm was over. Soon
Theseus and his friends could see land,
and then the city of Athens…
but nobody remembered
the ship's black sail.
Nobody remembered
to unroll a white
sail instead.

While Theseus was away, Aegeus thought about his son every day. In the evenings he climbed a high rock by the sea and watched for ships. Finally he recognised the Cretan ship. When it came closer, he could clearly see its black sail.

"My son, my son!" he cried. "The Minotaur has killed him!" Aegeus threw himself off the rock and into the water below. Even today, the sea where he disappeared is called the Aegean Sea.

Theseus and his friends arrived home, but they knew immediately that something was wrong. Why was the city so silent? No one smiled at them, and no one was singing or dancing in the streets, although all their children were home now and safe. They were confused – and then they heard the terrible news about Aegeus's death.

In time, Theseus became King of Athens. He was a good king, and a hero to his people, but they never forgot King Aegeus.

About the story

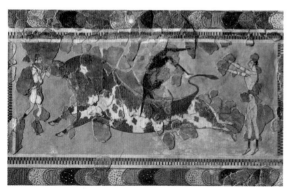

Thousands of years ago in Greece, long before there were books, people told stories about kings, queens, heroes and monsters. Storytellers listened to them, learned them and then told others. Later, people wrote the stories down, which is how we know them today.

Some parts of Theseus's story may be based on things that really happened. Around 120 years ago, archeologists (people who study objects from the past) found the ruins of a palace at Knossos on the island of Crete. It was like a maze, with lots of rooms. Pictures on the walls, like the one above, showed bulls with people jumping over them, either dancing or fighting. We can't be sure that Theseus and Ariadne were real, but the sea around Athens really is still called the Aegean.

Activities

The answers are on page 40.

Who says this?

Choose *two* sentences for each character.

Aegeus

Theseus

Ariadne

A.

When you see the white sail, you will know the good news.

B.

If I refuse, Minos will attack us again.

C.

Does my name ever go into the pots?

D.

Promise to take me with you when you leave the island.

E.

You are brave, I know that - but you are all I have.

F.

How could they forget me so soon?

Mixed-up story

Can you put these pictures and sentences in order?

A.

The king's soldiers took fourteen names from two enormous pots.

B.

"Come with me, quickly. I will take you to the Labyrinth."

C.

It fell to the floor and roared for the last time.

D.

"Keep the ball with you and unroll it as you go through the maze."

E.

That night, the Athenians had a surprise visitor.

F.

There was one ship that nobody in the city wanted to see.

G.

They sailed away into the dark before Minos could find out.

H.

In the middle of the maze, he found the monster.

I.

Everyone in Athens knew about Theseus's promise.

Say why

Choose the right ending for each sentence.

1.

Theseus went to his father Aegeus because...

A. ...he wanted to keep his name out of the pots.

B. ...he wanted to go to Crete and defeat the Minotaur.

2.

Aegeus and the Athenians watched silently because...

A. ...they knew this was their only chance.

B. ...they didn't believe Theseus.

3.

Ariadne wanted to help the Athenians because...

A. ...she felt terrible that they were going to die.

B. ...she wanted to annoy her father Minos.

4.

Theseus fell onto his knees because...

A. ...he really liked Ariadne.

B. ...he was exhausted.

What is Ariadne thinking?

Match the sentences to the pictures.

A.
I hope he will
be safe.

B.
How could he
be so cruel?

C.
What can I do
to help them?

D.
We should
stop and find
some water.

1.

2.

3.

4.

The end of the story

Choose a word to finish each sentence.

1.

Theseus soon saw his ....

friend   home   mistake

2.

Nobody .... the ship's black sail.

expected   remembered   touched

3.

In the evenings he climbed a .... rock by the sea.

heavy   high   horrible

4.

Why was the .... so silent?

city   palace   ship

Word list

attack (v) if you attack someone, you start
a fight with them or try to hurt them.

Athenian (n) a person who comes
from the city of Athens (Greece).

bull (n) a male cow.

confused (adj) when you don't understand something,
or you don't know what's happening, you are confused.

Cretan (n) a person who comes
from the island of Crete (Greece).

cruel (adj) a cruel person treats other
people badly and enjoys hurting them.

defeat (v) when you defeat someone,
you win a fight or a game against them.

demand (n, v) when you tell someone to give
you something or do something, and you
won't let them refuse, you make a demand.

entrance (n) the way in to a place.

exhausted (adj) extremely tired.

fresh (adj) clean, new. Fresh air is clean and pure.
Fresh water is good drinking water, not sea or salt water.

horns (n pl) the sharp points of bone on
an animal's head, such as a bull's head.

immediately (adv) very quickly and without waiting.

knee (n) the part that bends in the middle of your leg.

labyrinth (n) a kind of maze (see next page).

maze (n) a place with many paths where it is easy to get lost. Mazes can be buildings, or made of growing plants, or patterns on a paper that you can do as an activity.

only (only son/daughter) (adj) If you have just one child, you say you have an only child.

powerful (adj) very strong, or able to do things easily. A powerful king might be an important king with a large army of soldiers.

prison (n) usually a place for criminals. People in a prison are locked inside and cannot leave.

promise (v) when you promise something, you say something and then make sure it happens.

punish (v) if you punish someone, you make them suffer in some way for doing something wrong.

roar (n) a loud, angry sound, especially from a wild animal like a lion, a tiger or a bull.

sail (n, v) the large piece of cloth above a boat that catches the wind and makes it move forward; or to make a boat move by using a sail.

sailor (n) someone who sails a boat or ship.

silent (adj), **silently** (adv) without making a noise.

step (v) to move forward, starting to walk.

torch (n) a piece of wood, burning at one end to give light.

thread (n) you use thread to tie things together or to sew.

unroll (v) when you unroll something, you make it flat or loose or straight (when it has been in a ball or a bundle).

visitor (n) someone who visits a person or a place.

Answers

Who says this?
Aegeus - B, E
Theseus - A, C
Ariadne - D, F

Mixed-up story
F, A, I, E, B,
D, H, C, G

Say why
1B, 2A, 3A, 4B

What is Ariadne thinking?
1C, 2A, 3D, 4B

The end of the story
1. mistake
2. remembered
3. high
4. city

You can find information about other Usborne English Readers here:
usborne.com/englishreaders

Designed by Hope Reynolds
Series designer: Laura Nelson Norris
Edited by Mairi Mackinnon
Digital imaging: Nick Wakeford

Page 32: Bullfight, 1550-1450BC from the Palace of Knossos
© DeAgostini Picture Library/Scala, Florence.

First published in 2022 by Usborne Publishing Ltd.,
Usborne House, 83-85 Saffron Hill, London EC1N 8RT, England.
usborne.com Copyright © 2022 Usborne Publishing Ltd.

All rights reserved. No part of this publication may be reproduced, stored in a retrieval system or transmitted in any form or by any means without the prior permission of the publisher. The name Usborne and the Balloon logo are Trade Marks of Usborne Publishing Ltd. UE.